jF
CO

Cowley, Joy

The duck in the gun

DATE			

The DUCK in the GUN

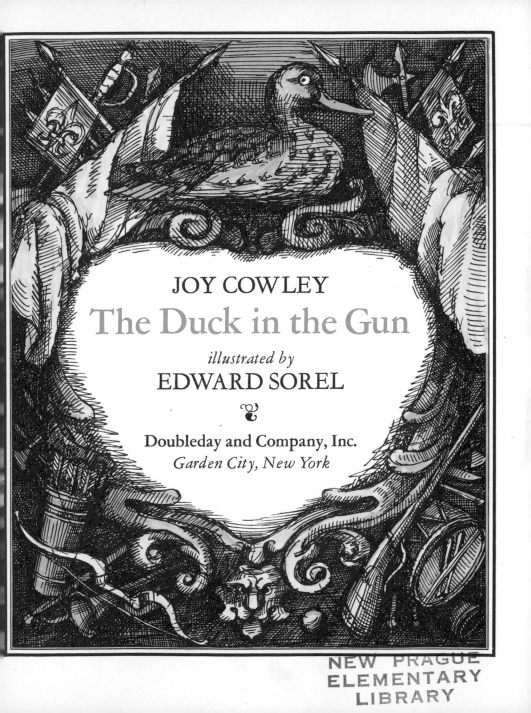

JOY COWLEY

The Duck in the Gun

illustrated by
EDWARD SOREL

Doubleday and Company, Inc.
Garden City, New York

Library of Congress Catalog Card Number 68–21885
Copyright © 1969 by Doubleday & Company, Inc.
All Rights Reserved
Printed in the United States of America
First Edition

For days the General and his men had been marching. Now they were all round the town and ready to fight.

The General called his Gunner.

"Is the gun in place?" he said.

"Yes, sir," said the Gunner.

"Is it aimed at the town?"

"Yes, sir," said the Gunner.

"Good," said the General. "Load it. When I give you the order, fire."

"Very well, sir," said the Gunner and he went away. But a little while later he came back. "Sir, we can't fire the gun."

"Why not?" shouted the General.

"Because we can't load it, sir."

The General grew red in the face. "Why can't you load it?" he shouted.

"Please, sir," said the Gunner. "There's a duck in the gun."

"A duck? In our gun?" The General jumped up from his chair.

"It has made a nest in there, sir."

"The cheek of it!" shouted the General. "It must go at once."

"I've tried, sir," said the Gunner, "but the duck won't come out. I think it is sitting on some eggs."

"Then I'll do something about it myself," said the General, picking up his sword. "I'll show that duck it can't stop an army."

The General and the Gunner went out to where the gun had been set, aimed at the town.

"You mean the duck's right in there?" said the General.

"Yes, sir," said the Gunner. "I put my hand in but I couldn't reach it."

The General looked down the gun and saw two small eyes looking back at him. "Here dilly, dilly, dilly," he called. "Nice dilly."

The duck said quack, quack, but didn't move.

The General's face went red again. "Come out, blast you!" he shouted and he banged on the gun with his sword.

There was another quack but the duck didn't stir from her nest.

"Please, sir," said the Gunner. "Could we put some food at the end of the gun? If the duck is hungry it'll come out and eat."

"A very good idea," said the General. "Get me some bread at once."

They put bits of fresh bread in the end of the gun but still the duck would not come out.

The General stamped up and down. "To think that a duck could upset my plans," he said.

"There is something you can do, sir," said one of the men. "You can fire it with the duck inside."

"No, no, no," said the General. "We'll think of something else. I know, we'll borrow a gun."

The General put on all his medals. Then he took a white flag and went to the town.

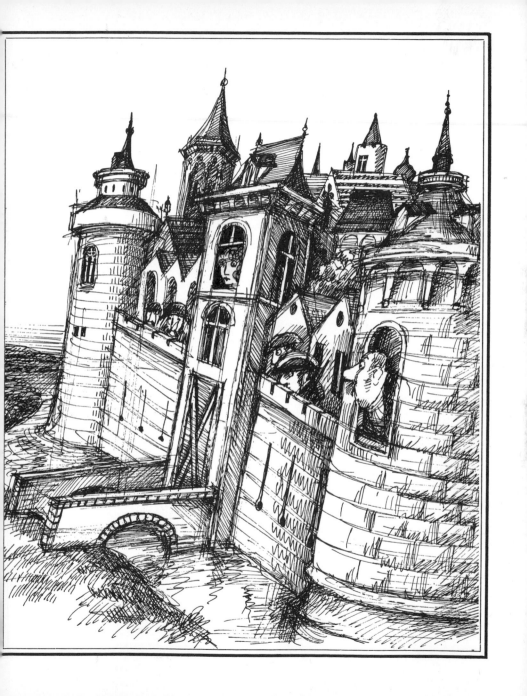

"Take me to your Prime Minister," he said to the town guards.

The guards led him through the streets to the Prime Minister's house. The General knocked on the door and at once it was opened by the Prime Minister's daughter.

"Good afternoon," said the General. "Do you know who I am?"

"Oh yes," said the girl, "I've seen your pictures in the paper. Won't you come in?" She turned away and called, "Father, here is the General to see you."

"How do you do," said the Prime Minister.

"Not very well," said the General, shaking his head. Then he told the Prime Minister about the duck in the gun.

"I see," said the Prime Minister. "And you can't really fire the gun with the duck inside. What are you going to do about it?"

The General coughed and looked at the floor.

"That's why I came to see you. I was wondering if you could lend us a gun. I mean, it's not very fair if you have guns and we haven't."

"Oh, I agree," said the Prime Minister. "But you see, we have only one gun."

"Couldn't we share it?" said the General. You could fire a shot at us; then we could take the gun and fire a shot at you."

The Prime Minister laughed. "Oh no. We can't let you have our gun. Besides, it is far too heavy to move."

For a while the General looked unhappy.

"It looks as though you'll have to put the war off for three weeks," said the Prime Minister. "By that time the duck will have hatched her eggs and you will have your gun back."

The General shook hands with the Prime Minister. "That's fair enough," he said. "We'll forget about the war for three weeks."

When the General's men heard the news they were very pleased. This meant they would have three weeks' holiday. In fact, they were so pleased that they put food down the gun whenever the General wasn't looking.

But after one week the General had another problem. He put on his medals, picked up his white flag and went to see the Prime Minister again.

"How are you?" said the Prime Minister.

"Not good at all," said the General. "The truth is, I'm running out of money. For a whole week my men have done nothing and they expect to be paid for it."

"That is a problem," said the Prime Minister.

"I don't suppose you could lend me some money," said the General.

"No," said the Prime Minister. "I can't give men money for doing nothing. But I can pay them if they will work for me. See our town? It needs painting. The houses are shabby and the shops look a mess. In two weeks your men could paint the whole town."

"What a great idea!" said the General. "Thanks very much. I'll tell my men at once."

This time the men were not so pleased. But when the General said he could no longer pay them, they agreed to work in the town.

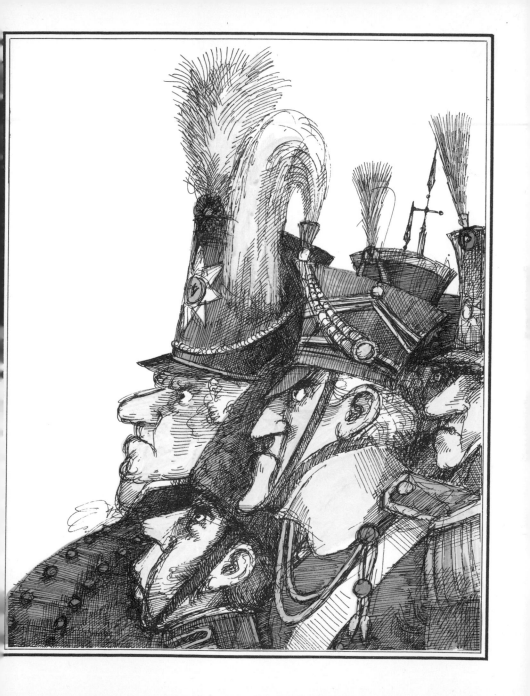

Early next morning they put on old clothes and left the camp. As soon as the last man had gone, the General went out to look at the gun. The duck was still there, sitting on her nest and quacking to herself. The General looked over his shoulder to

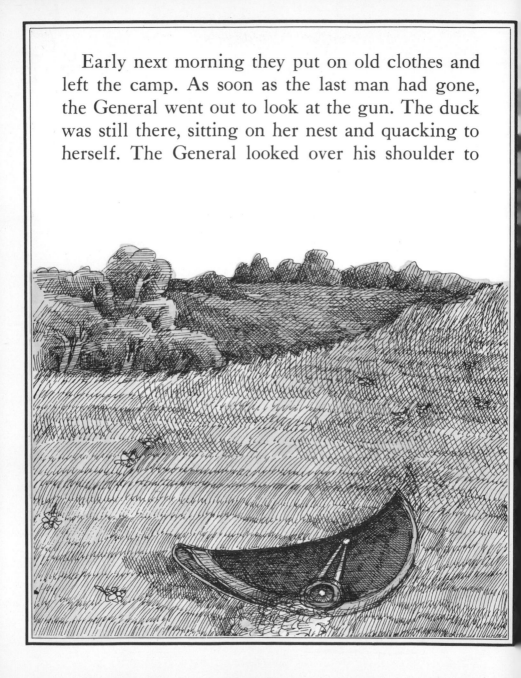

make sure that he was alone. He took some cake from his pocket, put it quickly down the gun and then went back to his tent. He spent the rest of the morning reading and lying in the sun.

Every day the men went to work in the town. It was very quiet at the camp. Sometimes the General would look at the town through his glasses and watch the houses change colour. Sometimes he visited the Prime Minister and his daughter and drank tea in their garden. Sometimes he would just walk as far as the gun with a pocket full of bread or biscuits.

Near the end of the third week the eggs hatched. The General went by the gun and heard not only quack, quack, but also a tiny beep, beep, beep.

The General rang the alarm bell as loudly as he could. At once the men put down their paints and brushes and ran back to camp.

"Attention!" called the General. "The duck's eggs have hatched." He looked inside the gun. "Here dilly, dilly," he called.

Out popped a little head. It was the first duck-

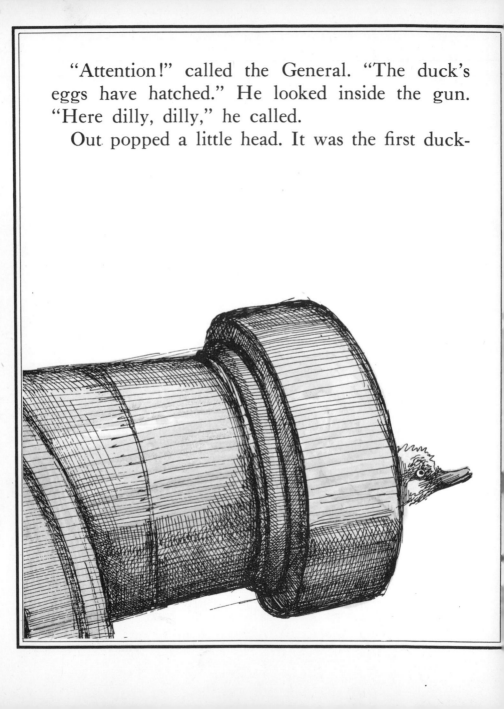

ling.

Very carefully, the General lifted it to the ground. Then another duckling came out, and another, until there were eight of them waddling round the

General's feet. Last out was the mother duck. She looked at all the men and quacked loudly. Then she flew down beside her ducklings and marched them off across the grass.

"Three cheers for the duck," shouted the men, throwing their hats in the air. "Hooray, Hooray, Hooray!"

"Now we can use our gun again," said the General. "At last we can have a war."

The men stopped cheering. They became very quiet. They stood with their hats in their hands and looked down at the ground.

"Please, sir," said the Gunner. "We can't shoot at that town. We would spoil the new paint."

"Yes," said the other men. "We've worked for two weeks on those houses."

The General nodded. It did seem silly to blow up freshly painted houses. Besides, he had become rather fond of the Prime Minister's daughter.

"What will we do, then?" he said.

"You couldn't put the war off for good, could you, sir?" said the Gunner. "After we've finished painting the town we can all go home."

The General thought for a long time. "All right," he said. "I'll go and tell the Prime Minister."

So that was the end of the war.

The men finished the painting in time to see the General marry the Prime Minister's daughter. It was a big wedding with flowers and bells and a cake that had a white sugar gun on top.

Of course the duck came. She and her eight duck-lings were there to march behind the army band.